JEWEL STICKER STORIES

The Magic Carousel Pony

Illustrated by Jerry Smath

To Kyle, Kendall, Rick & Jan

Grosset & Dunlap • New York

Once upon a time there was a girl named Carrie. Carrie loved ponies more than anything. Her room was filled with drawings of ponies. But Carrie didn't have a pony of her own. It made her very sad.

Pick out your favorite pony in Carrie's room and put a jewel sticker on it!

One day a carnival came to town. But Carrie
didn't care about the huge Ferris wheel, or the
cotton-candy machine, or the funny clowns.
All she cared about was the carousel. It played
beautiful music, and was filled with the most
dazzling ponies.

Decorate the lights on the Ferris wheel
with your jewel stickers.

"Step right up!" cried the ticket man. "Buy a ticket to ride the magic carousel!"

"Excuse me," said Carrie. "Is it really magic?"

The ticket man leaned over. "If you grab the gold ring, any wish you make will come true."

"Really?" said Carrie.

"Really," said the man. "Just you wait and see."

Put a jewel sticker on your favorite clown.

Carrie bought a ticket and right away she found the horse of her dreams. It was white, with a pink mane and tail and bright blue eyes. Carrie called her Sparkle, because she was covered in bright shiny jewels.

Decorate the carousel with jewel stickers.

Carrie rode Sparkle every day for a week. But try as she might, she could never reach the gold ring.

Finally, it was the last day of the carnival. Carrie sadly climbed up on Sparkle's back. The music began to play and the carousel went around and around. Carrie just had to get the gold ring. She leaned over as far as she could to try to reach it. Yes! The gold ring was hers!

Use your jewel stickers
to decorate Sparkle.

That night before Carrie fell asleep she started thinking.
Could the ticket man have been telling the truth? Carrie
held the gold ring tightly and closed her eyes. She wished
with all her might that Sparkle was her very own.

**Make the gold ring glow
with a jewel sticker.**

"Neigh!"

Carrie woke up with a start. Rubbing her eyes, she ran to the window and looked out. And there, standing in the backyard was Sparkle—her jeweled saddle shining in the moonlight.

"My wish came true!" said Carrie. "The ticket man was right!"

Make the moon brighter with a jewel sticker.

Still holding the gold ring, Carrie ran outside and climbed up on Sparkle's back. "Let's ride through town!" she suggested. Sparkle jumped over the backyard fence and off they went. They galloped down the street, past Carrie's best friend's house, and past her school.

Make the street lamps glow
with your jewel stickers.

Carrie looked up at the midnight sky filled with sparkling stars. "Oh, how I wish we could fly!" she said. Just then the gold ring began to glow. Before her very eyes, Sparkle sprouted a pair of beautiful glittery golden wings.

Decorate Sparkle's golden wings with your jewel stickers.

With a mighty leap, Sparkle took off into the air. They were flying! High above the rooftops they soared. "I see my house!" said Carrie. She thought for a moment. "Let's fly as high as the brightest star!" she said.

Up, up, up they flew until the houses below looked like a toy village.

Put a jewel sticker on
the brightest star of all.

But all too soon, the sky turned a rosy red. The sun
was coming up and it was time for Carrie to go home.

They landed in Carrie's backyard. Carrie climbed down. "Good-bye Sparkle, I'll never forget you," she whispered. Sparkle turned and nudged the gold ring. "You mean I can still use this?" asked Carrie. Sparkle whinnied in reply.

Do you see the sun peeking over the horizon? Mark it with a jewel sticker.

The next day the carnival was gone, but Carrie wasn't sad. She knew that all she had to do was hold her gold ring tightly and make a wish. And no matter how far away Sparkle was, she would come and take Carrie for a midnight ride to the stars.